PROJECT MANAGER & EDITOR
Tomas Härenstam

CO-PUBLISHER
Chris Birch

WRITERS
Torsten Alm (Lair of the Saurians), Petter Bengtsson (The Family Homestead),
Jonas Ferry (Seed of Evil), Mattias Lilja (The Oracle of the Silver Egg),
Tomas Härenstam (Long Journeys), Nils Karlén (Monster Generator)

COVER ART
Ola Larsson

INTERIOR ART & MAPS
Reine Rosenberg

GRAPHIC DESIGN
Christian Granath

LAYOUT & PREPRESS
Dan Algstrand

TRANSLATION
Martin Larsson

PROOFREADING
T.R. Knight

PRINT
Zenith Media

ISBN
978-1-910132-36-4

⌈01⌉

ZONE COMPENDIUM

Welcome to the first Zone Compendium for *Mutant: Year Zero*. This booklet contains plenty of material for you to use as a Gamemaster.

The bulk of the book consists of four *Special Zone Sectors*, scenario locations just like the ones in Chapter 15 of the core book. You can place the Special Zone Sectors in any section you want on the Zone map, for the PCs to discover and explore.

Each Special Zone Sector comes with a map in two versions:

▫ The GM map has several small images added. These show what is actually hidden inside the sector and thus gives you, as a GM, a good overview of the entire location. Don't show this version of the map to the players.
▫ The players' version of the map lacks these images and can therefore be shown to the players as soon as they enter the sector. The players' maps are collected at the end of the booklet, and they are all available for download from the Modiphius website.

After the Special Zone Sectors there is a section with rules on how to handle long journeys in the game. At the very end there is a very useful random Monster Generator that lets you create your own mutated beasts with just a few dice rolls.

If you have any questions or want to discuss the contents of this Zone Compendium with others, please visit the official forum at *modiphius.com/mutant*.

LAIR OF THE SAURIANS

In the depths of the Zone, by an islet in dark waters, rests a gigantic rusted metal tube. Zone Stalkers say it's an old underwater vessel. They say there are amazing artifacts in the tube, but that it is guarded by dangerous zone monsters. The PCs can come here on an expedition looking for treasure, or just happen to pass by during their treks through the Zone.

OVERVIEW

The small island, sticking out of a major body of water in the Zone, is overgrown by sinuous plants and stunted trees. The island could pass for any island in the Zone were it not for the ancient giant tube that has tried to wriggle its way onto the shore like a huge zone monster. The vessel is almost as long as the Ark, several mutants high and made from resilient, rusty metal from the Old Times. Only a few scrap crows circle the islet and the vessel would look uninhabited if not for the thin tendril of smoke rising from a cylinder-shaped tower halfway down the hull.

LOCATIONS

The metal tube is an old nuclear submarine. The ravages of time have destroyed most of its interior, but deep within the tube some treasures remain after all. The submarine is sectioned off by circular doors that are opened by twisting a large handle. Since the reactor of the sub is partly functional, flickering emergency lighting illuminate some compartments. The smell of fish and seaweed is strong throughout the vessel.

Tower: The submarine's tower serves as a watch-tower and is also the easiest way to get in and out of the submarine (at least for regular mutants that can't breathe under water, see below). There is always a guard here from the Saurians (below), and the PCs must roll Sneak (–2 in daylight) to get to the hull of the submarine undetected.

Fully functional diving gear (see page 193 of *Mutant: Year Zero*) can be found in a watertight metal locker. A hatch at the top of the tower leads to a cramped corridor that leads further down into the submarine's interior.

Bridge: A fairly large compartment lined with numerous broken glass screens and panels. In the middle of the room a massive pillar stretches from the floor and up into the tower. The floor is littered with scraps of paper and other odd gear.

The Saurians have propped their weapons against the wall. Spears, tridents, bows, quivers of arrows. Anyone that goes through the debris in the room can find a pair of binoculars (see page 191 of *Mutant: Year Zero*). The pillar in the middle of the room is a periscope that Dante, leader of the Saurians, uses to scout for enemies in the Zone.

Galley: A compartment filled with cabinets, benches and shelves made of rusted metal. Tidy rows of slimy, greenish eggs rest on the reeds that cover the floor. A drain pipe leads up from an oil drum at the end of the room to a hole in the hull. A fire in the oil drum keeps the area very warm.

In the galley is the artifact that could make the inhabitants of the submarine a future power-broker in the Zone: an ancient water purifier. This amazing device is too large and complicated to remove,

unfortunately, and it needs plenty of power to work. However, it can create 50 doses of rot free water every day, as long as the submarine remains in its current location.

The galley also contains a selection of kitchen related scrap (frying pan, cutting board, kitchen knife) and 1D6 rations of grub.

Mess hall: The submarine's mess hall is the main gathering place of the Saurians. Large parts of the tribe eat and sleep here. The reptiles have cleared out most of the furnishings. The floor is covered by woven reed mats. The smell of fish is very strong here.

Officers' mess: The old officers' mess serves as Dante's throne room. The alpha male's throne is built from the remains of an old tennis umpire's chair. Dante uses the score keeper to judge conflicts between members of the tribe. He spends most of his time here, usually to enjoy gifts from the tribe. Septina can usually be found by his side.

Captain's quarters: This compartment is decorated with all sorts of things, among others a dirty red flag and several maps of unknown areas. Adjacent to the room there is a shower stall and a toilet. The captain's quarters serve as Dante's bedchamber. The alpha male sleeps and mates in the ancient shower, which is still functioning sporadically. There are well-kept sea charts in the captain's quarters as well as some appropriate scrap (from the scrap table on page 262 of *Mutant: Year Zero*). The charts are equivalent to the artifact Map of the Zone (see page 196 of *Mutant: Year Zero*).

The officers' quarters are reserved for the highest ranking females in the tribe. The compartments are mostly empty but in a few of them there might be maritime scrap. To a regular mutant, a reptilian lair appears like a foul-smelling room filled with dried algae, seaweed and reeds.

The crew's berths are located in a corridor that runs down the length of the boat. The berths are hammocks securely fastened along the walls. Some of the most renowned of the tribe's warriors sleep here.

LAIR OF THE SAURIANS

TOWER

HATCH TO THE BRIDGE

ENGINE ROOM

REACTOR

CAPTAIN'S QUARTERS

TORPEDO ROOM

Hydrophone and radio room: A cramped compartment with advanced equipment along the right-hand bulkhead. The remains of an Ancient with headphones on occupy a chair. A gearhead can get the equipment up and running with a Demanding (–1) roll for Jury-Rig. Mostly all you hear is static but maybe you can get a bearing on something...

Engine room: A ladder leads down to the engine room at the back of the submarine. Most of the room is filled with rot contaminated water (one Rot Point per minute). The propeller shaft is broken clean off and a large hole in the hull leads out into the water below the submarine. The Saurians use the hole to exit and enter the submarine covertly.

Torpedo room: The torpedo room is at the bow of the submarine. Racks along the bulkhead held the vessel's arsenal. Now they are empty apart from two rusted old weapons. The torpedoes are stuck to the shelf and require an Insane (–3) roll for Force to dislodge. To move the torpedoes even a short distance without a vehicle or a cart requires a Hard (–2) roll for Force.

The torpedoes are powerful but bulky weapons. A gearhead can Jury-Rig them to make them operational again. They will have a Blast Power of 10.

The torpedo hatches are accessible via the launch tubes. One of the two hatches is open and leads up to the shore. The Saurians rarely visit the torpedo room and are unaware of the open tube.

Reactor: The reactor of the submarine is next to the engine room. The door to it is rusted shut and it would take advanced equipment or determined acts of violence (a total of 25 damage points) to open it. The reactor is leaking and the whole room has Rot Level 3 (one Rot Point per minute).

Lower storage area: The lower storage area is in the bow, underneath the torpedo room. Most of the space is flooded and the PCs have to swim (roll Move) through corridors under water to reach the door that leads into the storage area. The water is contaminated by Rot giving the PC one Rot Point. To reach the storage area, they have to force open a door that has been rusted shut, with a Hard (–2) roll

01

for Force. The passageway to the door can only hold one person at a time.

Once inside, the PCs will find what's left of the submarine's emergency provisions (see below). The PCs may also draw an Artifact Card if you want.

THE SITUATION

The submarine is the lair of a large group of Saurians. They have yet to understand what a remarkable discovery they have made there. Instead they have settled for living on the islet peacefully, at least compared to the rest of the Zone.

Rumors of the great vessel and the riches within have spread throughout the Zone. Until recently the Saurians have managed to kill or scare off any intruders, but a few days ago captain Ossian and his scrap pirates arrived. Ossian is a powerful presence in the Zone and with his scrap ship, *The Wrecker*, he spreads terror on its rot infested waters.

The scrap pirates' initial attack was met with fierce resistance and Ossian retreated after heavy losses. The pirates have nursed their wounds for a few days and laid plans for a new attack. Ossian and his men are skilled warriors but are outnumbered by the Saurians, who also have excellent defensive positions.

INHABITANTS

The Saurians are mutated, intelligent reptilians of unknown origin. They never lived in an Ark, they have been in the submarine for several generations. They are short, most of them only slightly over a meter tall, and have greenish leathery skin.

The reptiles are all born as females, but can change sex as needed. There is only one male in the tribe, and he is their leader. If the male dies or shows weakness, the strongest female changes sex. During the transformation, she withdraws to a secluded cranny. When he returns to the tribe as a male, he challenges the current dominant male, and the loser is forced to leave the tribe.

Dante is the current leader of the Saurians. He is tall, almost two meters, with a powerful build. He wears a green army jacket. An ancient assault rifle is slung over his shoulder. Dante's goals are to expand the tribe and build a permanent settlement on the island. Dante looks down on anyone who is not of the Saurians and is a tough negotiator. If a situation would turn bad for the flock, Dante is very pragmatic. He tries to save his own skin, if he is unable to do so he will try to negotiate his way out of the situation.

Attributes: Strength 4, Agility 4, Wits 3, Empathy 3.
Skills: Command 4, Fight 3, Move 3, Shoot 3, Manipulate 3.
Armor: 3

Gear: Assault rifle (see page 191 in *Mutant: Year Zero*), backpack, entrenching shovel (equivalent to Blunt object), Zippo lighter, 3D6 bullets.

Septina is the dominant female of the tribe. She is the informal leader of the tribe and is feared by all its members. Septina despises Dante's weakness and is waiting for the right opportunity to push him out. Septina wears a t-shirt and fights fiercely with a saw-toothed artifact.

Attributes: Strength 5, Agility 2, Wits 3, Empathy 2.
Skills: Command 3, Fight 4, Move 2, Shoot 2.
Armor: 3
Gear: Chainsaw (see page 192 of *Mutant: Year Zero*), crossbow (see page 193 of *Mutant: Year Zero*), can of gasoline, eight arrows.

Reptile warriors: Apart from Dante and Septina, the tribe consists of around 50 females, from tiny hatchlings to old scarred reptiles. Even the fully grown female warriors are fairly short, around 130 centimeters.

Attributes: Strength 3, Agility 3, Wits 1, Empathy 1.
Skills: Fight 2, Shoot 3, Shoot 2.
Armor: 3
Gear: Fishing spear or trident (equivalent to scrap spear), bow or slingshot, four arrows.

TRAITS OF THE SAURIANS
The Saurians are a form of beast mutant (see page 171 of *Mutant: Year Zero*) and have no mutations. They do have other abilities, however:

- They are immune to Rot up to level 2.
- They have double rows of razor sharp teeth and long talons (damage 2, Gear Bonus 0).
- They can spit acid (damage 1, range Near, roll Shoot).
- They can stay up to 15 minutes under water.
- They speak a very primitive and feral form of the language the PCs speak. A successful Comprehend roll is required to communicate with them.

Captain Ossian: A tall, thin and weather-beaten man with wild black hair and beard, peppered with grey. Ossian's goal is to become ruler of the Zone and he will stop at nothing to achieve this. He is not a coward but is not reckless. In the heat of battle, he stays in the background. He alternates between extremely ingratiating and threatening, and is always trying to manipulate those around him. Sometimes he roars with laughter for no apparent reason. The PCs may run into him at other locations in the Zone. Maybe at Rust Castle or with The Helldrivers (see chapter 15 of *Mutant: Year Zero*).

Attributes: Strength 4, Agility 5, Wits 3, Empathy 4.
Skills: Find the Path 2, Command 4, Fight 3, Move 3, Shoot 4, Comprehend 4, Sense Emotion 2, Manipulate 4.
Talents: Coward.
Mutations: Human Magnet, Parasite, 5 MP.
Artifact: Compass (see page 192 of *Mutant: Year Zero*)
Gear: Cutlass, scrap pistol (11 bullets), eight rations of grub, two rations of water, bottle of booze, Captain Hook action figure (lucky charm).

Scrap pirates: Large and heavy mutants in ragged clothes. The scrap pirates are close to desperate since their food and water supplies are running low. Currently there are 17 able combatants on The Wrecker.

Attributes: Strength 4, Agility 4, Wits 2, Empathy 1.
Skills: Fight 2, Move 2, Shoot 3, Comprehend 2.
Mutations: One random mutation, 2 MP.
Gear: Cutlass or scrap knife, scrap pistol or scrap rifle, 1D6 bullets, 1D6 rations of grub, 1D6 rations of water.

ARTIFACTS
There are plenty of valuable artifacts onboard the old submarine:

- Diving gear in the tower
- Binoculars on the bridge
- Sea charts in the captain's quarters
- Torpedoes in the torpedo room
- One random artifact in the lower storage area
- Water purifier in the galley (above)

The scrap pirates also have the scrap ship, The Wrecker, and a motorboat. If you do not want to give these kinds of artifacts to the PCs make sure they are destroyed in the battle with the Saurians.

GRUB, WATER AND BULLETS

The reptiles have a container with 60 rations of rot free water next to the water purifier.

Grub is very scarce. The Saurians sustain themselves by hunting and do not cook their food. There are a few old boxes of canned food (2D6 rations of rot free grub and 3D6 of rot contaminated grub) in the lower storage area. There are also 3D6 bullets in an ammunition box there.

The scrap pirates are low on grub and water. There is no more water than what each pirate is carrying. The same goes for bullets.

EVENTS

When the PCs arrive at the islet a sense of calm permeates the area. They probably need to construct some sort of floatation device to be able to reach the island. If their party doesn't include a competent gearhead, you can let them find a scrap raft in the reeds on the shore. Maybe a pirate lies dead on it, several arrows protruding from his body. Once on the islet, you can let the PCs sneak around a bit (maybe they are attacked by scrap crows who make their nests there) before things start happening.

- The Saurians mistake the PCs for scrap pirates. They sneak up on the intruders and attack as they approach the submarine. The PCs can fight or attempt to negotiate – the latter requires a successful Comprehend to understand the language and then a successful Manipulate.
- At an appropriate moment – in the middle of the fight between the PCs and the reptiles or just as the negotiations are about to bear fruit – The Wrecker emerges from the zone smog. The scrap pirates attack! Let the PCs act however they want to. Will they pick a side, or will they take advantage of the situation in some other way?

THE WRECKER

The Wrecker is an old car ferry from the Old Times (of the type that transports vehicles across lakes). A few car wrecks and a number of tents that serve as dwellings for the pirates occupy the deck. Ossian has his lair on the bridge, where there is a robust scrap cannon mounted. The cannon is operated by the gearhead Gros (use the template for scrap pirate, add Jury-Rig 2). Currently there are four loads for the cannon.

When Ossian isn't onboard it is first mate Erje that has command over the ferry. The ferry counts as a Ship (see page 109 of *Mutant: Year Zero*). On one end of the ferry Gros has built a liquor still. Currently there is half a barrel of liquor. The pirates also own a number of scrap rafts and a motor boat (see page 196 of *Mutant: Year Zero*).

The Wrecker can also be used for the Event A Beacon in the Distance (see page 134 of *Mutant: Year Zero*) before the PCs run into the island of the Saurians.

- The pirates do not fight till their last breath. They retreat again once they have caused the reptiles enough harm. Ossian's plan is to grind down their resistance and wear the reptiles out.
- If the PCs haven't taken the pirates' side openly, Dante attempts to recruit them to his cause. Dante views the alliance as temporary, but can be persuaded to enter into a more permanent agreement.
- Dante wants the PCs to infiltrate the scrap pirates and kill Ossian. He offers artifacts from the submarine as a reward.
- Ossian is also open to an alliance with the PCs. They can seek him out on The Wrecker, which always lurks near the island, or Ossian can seek out the PCs. He views them as a means to an end and will betray them as soon as they have served his purposes. Enforcers

and Gearheads could possibly be offered a permanent place among the pirates.
- The scrap pirates attack the Saurians again. The pirates fight without mercy. If the PCs are on their side they are forced to witness the pirates killing everyone, adults and children, indiscriminately. This might be the time to switch sides.
- Septina decides it's time to challenge Dante over leadership of the tribe. She withdraws to her cabin or a secluded place on the islet and starts her transformation to male. Dante realizes what is about to happen. If the PCs are on his side he encourages them to seek her out and kill her before she challenges him.
- If no one stops Septina she challenges Dante to a duel. The PCs, with or without the pirates, can take this opportunity to attack the reptiles, or simply loot the submarine. They can also try to mediate between Dante and Septina and unite the reptiles against the pirates.

THE ORACLE OF THE SILVER EGG

Zone Stalkers say the man in the silver egg out in the swamp knows the answers to any question. They say he can even show the way to Eden. But they also warn any and all that the price for using his service is high – changes to body and soul, if you come back at all.

OVERVIEW

In a swamp in the Zone a large silvery cone rises from the marshy ground. Footbridges above the stagnant water lead from scrap sheds to the ancient wonder. The egg, as the Zone Stalkers call it, is known as the lair of the oracle Zakarya. Some say he can see the future, others say that he bestows luck upon his visitors and others believe he is evil incarnate.

People from all over the Zone travel here to leave grub and water for Zakarya in exchange for his prophecies, but they generally make sure not to stay too long. A band of mutants have taken it upon themselves to guard the area and administrate visitations and gifts to the oracle. They call themselves Guardians of the Egg and are led by the zealous Greglas.

LOCATIONS

The silver egg is a space pod from the space station belonging to the Titan Power Mimir. The pod is built with enclave technology, and its innards are mostly incomprehensible to the PCs. The pod's energy source is a fission reactor, and all technology except the engine itself is functional. Since the fission reactor is under water a perpetual fog surrounds the pod, created by the reactor's heated inner processes.

Camp site: A group of tents where the oracle's visitors can camp occupy an open area close to the egg. On an average day there are a handful of visitors there. The tents surround a central fire pit.

The dwellings of the Guardians: The Guardians of the Egg have built their dwellings out in the marsh on stilts. Simple sheds built from scrap and reeds are reached by wooden footbridges. A large bridge leads up to the Egg itself. In the waters under the sheds a Rotfish lurks (see page 181 of *Mutant: Year Zero*). She lives on refuse but wouldn't mind a bite of any mutant that falls into the water...

Greglas' dwelling: The leader of the Guardians keeps his house sparsely furnished and it contains no valuables apart from some grub and water. Greglas is described in detail on page 14.

Danianna's dwelling: The floor of this scrap shed is covered by skins of zone monsters that the warrior woman has vanquished. The tusks of a Razorback hang on one wall and ornaments made of bone and feathers hang from the ceiling. The shed contains no valuables.

The Place of Gifts: In the front of the pod's hatch, the Guardians have built a platform where Greglas, seated behind an ancient school desk, keeps a ledger of all the visitors. He notes the visitor's name in an ancient black book and hands them a metal plaque with a number etched into it. Next to the desk is a big steel chest on wheels. All the gifts to the oracle are kept in the chest – mostly it's filled with scrap but also 1D6 rations of grub and rot free water.

Antechamber: The pod's hatch opens automatically with a hissing sound. Inside is a cramped chamber with white walls and blinking panels, with mystic symbols of various colors daubed here and there.

Whoever enters the antechamber is enveloped by a cloud of gas, sprayed from pipes in the ceiling and walls. The cloud instantly sanitizes the visitor from all non-permanent Rot (roll as usual to see if some Rot becomes permanent). Feel free to use the sanitation cloud to scare the players!

In the middle of the chamber, a ladder leads up and down. The ladder going up leads to the control room. The ladder going down leads to two levels – the first with a lounge, sleeping chamber and med-lab, the second with engine room, cryochamber and docking chamber.

If the PCs are invited in, the oracle's voice emanates from hidden speakers, encouraging them to climb up the ladder, to the control room. All the chambers have doors that open with a push of a button on the wall next to them. If the oracle has invited them he opens the doors in their path, otherwise the PCs have to roll Comprehend to open them. Once they have succeeded, they don't have to roll again.

Control room: A large chamber filled with strange devices and blinking panels. A throne-like chair that rotates 180 degrees is in the center of the chamber. The walls are covered with symbols similar to those in the antechamber. Ornaments and carvings made of bone and feathers hang from the ceiling (gifts for the oracle). Next to the throne, the oracle has placed a gas canister with sedatives from the med-lab (below) and a respiratory mask. The canister contains 1D6 doses of the gas.

The video screens in the room are connected to cameras and microphones in every chamber of the pod. There are also controls for the external communication equipment of the pod. Zakarya has destroyed them. A skilled gearhead can fix it (Jury-Rig –2) – perhaps you can get a bearing on something?

Lounge: This chamber has a small kitchenette and an elliptical table surrounded by six stools. Both the table and the stools are bolted to the floor. The whole chamber is splattered with blood. A large

screen that can show surveillance images from the pod and its surroundings occupies one wall. Zakarya uses the chamber as a kill room.

2D6 rations of grub and the same amount of rot free water can be found in a refrigerator.

Sleeping chamber: At the top of the pod there is a small room with six bunks and lockers of personal belongings. The lockers are empty apart from some clothes (simple jumpsuits with the symbol of the Titan Power Mimir), a photograph of a woman and a suitable artifact. The room is completely white and feels very sterile. Zakarya has programmed Multi to keep the room clean.

Medlab: A compact sick bay. There is medical equipment here that adds +3 to a roll of Heal to treat whoever is injured – but only in the lab itself, and the PC that uses Heal must first Comprehend the equipment.

Here the PCs can also find sedatives, painkillers and stimulants – one dose heals 1D6 Fatigue (Agility), Damage (Strength) and Confusion (Wits) respectively, but they must be administered using a respiratory mask that can be found in the medlab. There are 2D6 doses of each drug. The sedatives and painkillers are hallucinogenic and will cause an equal amount of Confusion (Wits) to the Agility or Strength they heal.

Engine room: A room filled with humming machinery, completely incomprehensible to the PCs. The machine creature Multi spends most of its time in this room.

Cryochamber: A chamber with six beds covered by glass cowls. Each bed has a panel with blinking lights and displays. The cryobeds were used to stabilize very sick or severely injured individuals. They are still working – a mutant who is injured and placed in a cryobed won't die until he or she is awakened again. The PCs can't possibly figure this out through any other way than testing the beds, or if Zakarya should tell them for some reason.

THE ORACLE
OF THE SILVER EGG

CONTROL ROOM

SLEEPING CHAMBER

CRYOCHAMBER

Docking chamber: The chamber is dominated by a strange wheeled vehicle. One of its axles is broken but other than that it seems functional. There are six space suits in recessed lockers in one wall. A panel with buttons is on the far wall. A PC can use Comprehend to realize that the buttons will open a ramp that leads outside the pod. Zakarya uses the ramp to dump his victims in the swamp.

ENCLAVE TECHNOLOGY

The pod that the oracle lives in is a result of the hyper advanced technology that the Titan Powers developed after the Apocalypse. Most of it is incomprehensible to the PCs. Describe it as mysterious and frightening. Enclave technology is very rare in *Mutant: Year Zero* but will be described in more detail in upcoming supplements. Some simple functions can be understood using Comprehend, like opening doors with the push of a button. The following artifacts are those the PCs could understand:

Space suit: A suit used for operations outside the atmosphere. The suit gives a Protection rating 12 against the Rot, but is very cumbersome to move around in. The wearer has to roll Endure each time he does something strenuous. DEV Requirement: Technology 50. DEV Bonus: Technology +1D6.

Chain knife: A highly effective, electrically powered chain knife, perfect to cut your way through thick Zone vegetation. The saw can be used for approximately a week before it needs recharging (from a generator, for example). Gear Bonus +2, Damage 3, light weapon. DEV Requirement. Technology 40. DEV Bonus Technology +1D6.

Lunar rover: An electric mini car perfect for travelling through rough terrain. The battery lasts for a few hours. DEV Requirement: Technology 50. DEV Bonus: Technology +1D6.

LOUNGE

THE SITUATION

Zakarya is actually a non-mutated human who participated in an expedition sent by the Titan Power Mimir. The mission of the six members was to track down Doctor Retzius and Project Eden (see page 231 of *Mutant: Year Zero*), who left Mimir's space station and landed on Earth several years earlier.

Zakarya had latent mental problems and the meeting with the poisoned surface of the planet triggered a massive psychosis. He decided the group should stay on Earth forever. Once they had given up hope of finding any signs of Retzius and wanted to return home, Zakarya lost control. He murdered the whole crew in a fit of rage.

The mutated inhabitants of the Zone discovered the silver space pod in the swamp and were convinced it was divine. Zakarya realized he could take advantage of this. He used his technical skills to help visitors in exchange for company, food and water. He used the hallucinogenic gases from the med lab to drug the visitors and give them visions.

Zakarya was happy for a while, but his psychotic episodes resumed, stronger than ever. He came to believe that he was a god, and that the mutants were his subjects. His thirst for blood resurfaced and during a visit he killed a guest who questioned his prophecies. To hide the murder he created a myth that certain chosen visitors could reach a higher plane of existence and reach Eden. The ploy worked and raised the mythical status of the oracle even higher. Zakarya has begun murdering chosen visitors, and sinks their bodies in the swamp.

INHABITANTS

The player characters can meet a motley bunch of visitors in the camp. The rumor of the oracle has reached far and a place in line to meet the oracle is highly desirable. You can have the PCs meet Helldrivers, Mechies, Nova cultists and even Zone-Ghouls (see chapter 13 of *Mutant: Year Zero*). Below are descriptions of the main characters of the sector:

Zakarya was a scientist who was destined for a brilliant career in astrophysics. After killing his colleagues he has become more and more psychotic. At first he was wracked with guilt over his misdeeds, but encountering the Zone and taking the role as the oracle has worsened his state of mind considerably. Zakarya is now a full-blooded psychopath.

Attributes: Strength 3, Agility 5, Wits 5, Empathy 2.
Skills: Fight 4, Move 3, Shoot 2, Sense Emotion 4, Manipulate 5.
Mutations: Non-mutated.

Gear: Chain knife (see boxed text on enclave technology), protective suit (Protection Rating 3 against both physical damage and the Rot), gas canister with sedative gases and a facial mask (Heavy, D6 doses, see above for effects).

Multi: A spider-like robot, half a meter high, that climbs around in and on the pod, carrying out service work and repairs. Multi can also fix injured people. The robot follows routine programming unless Zakarya controls it directly from the control room. Multi can't speak but actually has a personality. The robot is very troubled by Zakarya's behavior but cannot act on it because of its programming. Communicating with the robot requires a roll of Comprehend with a modification of −2.

Attributes: Strength 3, Agility 6.
Skills: Fight 2, Move 4, Heal 5, Jury-Rig 5.
Armor: 6

Weapon: Welding laser (damage 1).

Greglas: A mutant severely contaminated by Rot. He has come to the silver egg to die and has taken the responsibility of dealing with newcomers and taking care of the gifts for the oracle. Greglas' responsibility is handling the line of visitors to the Oracle, where they get a metal plaque with a number etched into it. Greglas is completely unaware of Zakarya's true background and insanity. He believes, like the others, that the oracle truly has the power of prophecy.

Attributes: Strength 1, Agility 3, Wits 4, Empathy 2.
Skills: Move 2, Manipulate 3, Sense Emotion 4.
Mutations: Puppeteer, 4 MP.

Artifact: Umbrella

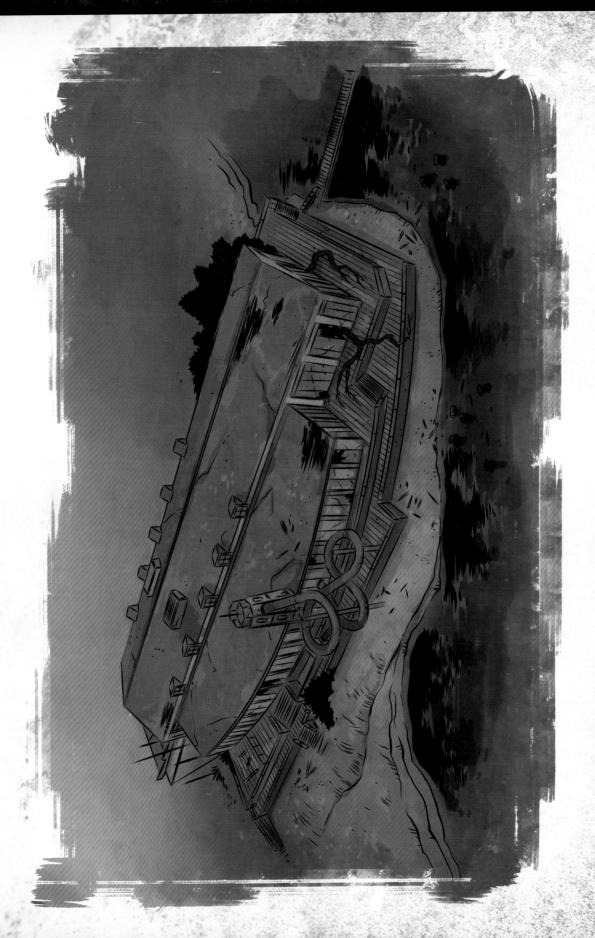

01

PLAYER MAP 3: ABANDONED BATHHOUSE

PLAYER MAP 4: THE FAMILY HOMESTEAD

Danianna: Young warrior from a nearby tribe of wild mutants. She was sent to the egg to meditate as part of her initiation rites. Greglas saw her potential and made her a Guardian of the Egg.

Attributes: Strength 4, Agility 4, Wits 3, Empathy 2.
Skills: Fight 3, Move 2, Shoot 3.
Mutations: Extreme Reflexes, 3 MP.
Gear: Scrap spear, bow, 8 arrows.

Guardians of the Egg: Mutated women and men who have been chosen by Greglas to guard and maintain the pod's surroundings. A lot of their time is spent keeping the pod spotless. The Guardians of the Egg will fight to the death to protect the oracle, Greglas and the pod.

Attributes: Strength 3, Agility 3, Wits 2, Empathy 2.
Skills: Fight 2, Move 1, Shoot 2.
Mutations: One random mutation, 3 MP.
Gear: Scrap spear, bow, four arrows.

ARTIFACTS

Artifacts the PCs can understand are scarce in the pod, apart from the enclave gadgets described in the boxed text on page 13. These all have a limited lifespan since the PCs cannot possibly repair them.

GRUBB, WATER AND BULLETS

There is usually some grub and Rot free water in the form of gifts for the oracle (1D6 rations of each) in the Place of Gifts. Down in the lounge there's a storage space with another 2D6 rations of each.

EVENTS

The PCs can come to the Silver Egg because they want to visit the oracle themselves – perhaps to look for a clue about Eden – or because they are looking for someone else who has gone here. They can also find the sector by coincidence.

- Those that wish to visit the oracle must first pay five bullets or something else of equivalent value to Greglas. Bargaining is possible. After this, the visitor gets a plaque with his number in line etched into it. The oracle meets with no more than 3–4 people per day. Group visits are not allowed.
- The PCs bump into an old friend or enemy at the camp site. Perhaps it's someone from the Ark or from another Zone sector.
- When a PC is next in line to visit the oracle she or he discovers that the metal plaque is gone. Someone has stolen it. Who?
- The PCs are hired discreetly to force the oracle to find out what happened to a friend of the employer. The friend visited the oracle some time ago and has not returned.
- A PC gets an audience with the oracle. Zakarya guides him to the control room using the speakers. The oracle mumbles and screams and stares intensely at the visitor. After a while he tells the PC to breathe "the magical air of the Ancients" through a mask connected to a gas canister. The canister contains a hallucinogenic sedative gas (see the medlab above for effects). If the PC refuses the oracle throws him out. If the PC gets violent Zakarya defends himself with his power saw, and the Guardians of the Egg rush in to his defense.
- If the PC breathes the oracle's air of the Ancients and is Broken by Confusion (Wits reaches zero), the oracle attempts to murder him ritually in the lounge. If the PC does not have a mutation that can save him, he should have an opportunity to save himself in some other way. Perhaps the other PCs notice what is about to happen. Perhaps something happens that diverts Zakarya's attention. Perhaps Multi recognizes an opportunity to stop the oracle and uses stimulants to wake the PC up?
- If the PC is not broken by Confusion he gets a massive buzz and experiences colorful visions of a future that probably won't happen. Go crazy with the descriptions!
- One of the PCs witnesses Zakarya dumping a dead body through the hatch in the dock. It's a mutant that visited the oracle a few days ago. He has not returned.

01

SEED OF EVIL

A tree suffering from megalomania is threatening the Ark. The tree is a killer tree that sends its bizarre seed pods, who can mimic the appearance of mutants, to the Ark. The pods lure victims away and feed them to the tree. The tree's goal is to use the nourishment available in the Ark to create enough seed pods to take over and control the whole Zone.

This zone sector is special. The location of the killer tree can be anywhere in the Zone, but the story begins in the Ark. It is possible to use the location of the tree independently, without the infiltration of the Ark, but the zone sector is much more striking if NPCs the PCs encountered in the Ark have been replaced by seed pods.

OVERVIEW

The killer tree lairs at the bottom of a drained 25 meter pool in an abandoned bathhouse. The building itself is massive and built of brick. A covered water slide snakes along the outside of the building and in through the wall to a drained pool. The walls in the lobby are tiled in artful patterns. There are identical sets of dressing rooms, with showers, a sauna and toilet, and an abandoned gym.

In the main hall there is a large 25 meter pool with a diving tower with springboards at one, three and five meters. The roots of the killer tree have broken through the tiles on the bottom of the drained pool. There's a kiddie pool, also drained, and along one wall of the hall there are wooden bleachers.

The tree is guarded by four seed pods in their natural form.

THE SITUATION

The zone Stalker Mirak unknowingly brought the first seed pod to the Ark. She camped outside the killer tree's bathhouse on her way home through the Zone. Her companion, the slave Bokk, was abducted in the night by a seed pod. The pod assumed Bokk's appearance, fed him to the tree and then accompanied Mirak on her journey. Another seed pod in its natural form followed Mirak and Bokk to the Ark.

Once they were back in the Ark, pod Bokk managed to lure the Boss Brutus to a secluded spot, where the second pod assumed his form. Pod Brutus had his gang capture mutants that he brought through the Zone to the tree to feed on, and has also gone out into the Zone with a gang member, a trip from which he returned alone. Pod Brutus no longer makes any other necessary decisions. The gang is getting restless and restless gangs are dangerous to others around them.

The Gearhead Urania is a member of the gang, but not a popular one. She is the only survivor of a rival gang. Brutus protected Urania as a reward for her help in bringing down the other boss, but the rest of the gang despise her. When Brutus was replaced by a pod her protection was gone. Urania is looking for help outside the gang.

Recently, a seed pod assumed the form of the Fixer Ester. Ester ran a store in the Ark, selling everything from tools to herbs, and pod Ester is still doing so. Since pod Ester has only worn Ester's form a short while, she has a great deal of her mutant personality left and isn't sure whether she is a mutant or a pod.

A pod that has assumed the form of a mutant can be discovered since they speak monotonously and without feelings, and they bleed white sap. They drink a lot of water, rot free or not, and always seek out sunlight. These traits are not noticeable at first, but grow more visible as the pod grows older. Pods from this particular killer tree also smell of nuts, more and more as the pod grows older.

INHABITANTS

The Killer Tree: The tree's goals cannot be heard in the rustle of its branches or be read in its bark, it can only be seen in the struggle of the pods to lure unsuspecting victims to become nourishment for the tree. It is not actively trying to spread and spawn new trees, but if a pod falls without being completely destroyed a new tree might sprout. The killer tree exudes a powerful numbing nutty smell.

Attributes: see Killer Tree on page 179 in *Mutant: Year Zero*.

Four seed pods: Armed with cutlasses, they defend the killer tree. The four pods are in their natural form, humanoid, but smooth, green, odorless and without facial features. They stay close to the tree, but can also be found patrolling the bathhouse or travelling to the Ark to procure more victims for the tree.

Attributes: See seed pod on page 179 of *Mutant: Year Zero.*

Gear: Cutlass

The Stalker Mirak: Provides the Ark with grub and scrap. Mirak's hair is as short as she can cut it on her own with a pair of scissors. She wears a heavy coat to protect herself from the weather in the Zone. She is passionate about the Ark and does whatever she can to help its inhabitants to a better life.

Attributes: Strength 2, Agility 5, Wits 3, Empathy 2.

Skills: Find the path 3, Shoot 2, Sneak 1.

Mutations: One random mutation, 3 MP.

Gear: Scrap rifle.

Bokk the Slave: A very old seed pod. Bokk was a small man, with tufts of hair and bad teeth. He was a slave belonging to Mirak, but in the Ark he would carry out any tasks the other inhabitants gave him. After Mirak's and Bokk's zone expeditions, he would push a shopping cart filled with scrap around, from which the people of the Ark could take whatever they needed. These days he spends his time rooted into place, shopping cart beside him, in the most open and sunny place in the Ark to absorb sunlight. He moves slowly and if he ever answers when spoken to he speaks incoherently. Bokk smells strongly of nuts.

Attributes: See seed pod on page 179 of *Mutant: Year Zero.*

Gear: Shopping cart filled with scrap.

Brutus the Boss: An old seed pod. Brutus was a large mutant, with dark hair and a full beard. He was loud, laughed raucously and brooked no argument when dispensing orders to his gang. As a seed pod he is very uncomfortable in any social setting. He avoids taking any decisions and laughs briefly and nervously. If he is put under any kind of pressure he sweats white sap. Pod Brutus smells of nuts.

Attributes: See seed pod on page 179 of *Mutant: Year Zero.*

Brutus' gang: Ten gang members, for now. Brutus uses the gang members to capture mutants few will

miss in the Ark. He personally takes the victim to the killer tree waiting in the depths of the Zone, or to a pod waiting outside the Ark to take the victim away. When the gang failed to find a suitable victim, Brutus took one of the gang members instead. Since the gang member never returned, the other members believe he was punished and have been unable to work up the courage to rebel against their boss.

Attributes: Strength 3, Agility 3, Wits 3, Empathy 3.

Skills: Any one skill at Skill level 2.

Gear: Scrap knife or spiked bat.

Urania the Gearhead: A member of Brutus' gang. Urania is one of the tallest mutants in the Ark and very thin. She has fair hair, bordering on translucent, and her forehead is covered by an irregular mark she has had since birth. Urania's specialties are engines and electricity, but she rarely gets to use them. Since Brutus is no longer protecting her she fears for her life, but knows she can't leave Brutus and his gang on her own.

Attributes: Strength 2, Agility 2, Wits 5, Empathy 3.

Skills: Jury Rig 3, Comprehend 2, Scout 1.

Mutations: One random mutation, 3 MP.

ABANDONED BATHHOUSE

GYM

DRESSING ROOM

KILLER TREE

Ester the Fixer: A new seed pod. Ester has red hair in a braid down her neck. She ran a small store in her den and continues to do so as a pod. Her assimilation was so complete that she still does not know that she is in the body of a pod, but her pod traits are becoming clearer by the day. Ester smells faintly of nuts.

Attributes: See seed pod on page 179 of *Mutant: Year Zero*.

The Gamemaster has the opportunity to spread paranoia both through false seed pods that turn out to be regular mutants, and by having more seed pods infiltrate the Ark. For extra effect, a pod could take the place of an NPC the PCs has interacted with before. Maybe there has been a slow replacement of mutants and now there are more pods than mutants? For every pod that is discovered the body count at the end of the gaming sessions is increased by one.

ARTIFACTS
Inside the bathhouse up to three random artifacts can be found.

GRUB, WATER AND BULLETS
There is no grub, water or bullets in the killer tree's lair. If all goes well however, there will be a lot of firewood.

EVENTS
- Mirak has promised the PCs scrap that they need, from her latest trip into the zone. Bokk has not shown up with his cart despite the fact that he and Mirak returned to the Ark several days ago. The PCs find pod Bokk in the sunniest place in the Ark. He barely speaks to them.
- Urania comes looking for the PCs and informs them that Brutus is acting oddly. She asks them to talk to him to try and figure out what's wrong.
- If the PCs ask Mirak, she allows them to examine Bokk. She also tells them about how they spent the night by the bathhouse. She never entered the building, she can only describe its exterior. Mirak offers to lead the

PCs to the site to save the Ark from being overrun by the pods.

◘ An NPC the PCs know disappears without a trace. If the PCs ask around several members of Brutus' gang turn up and try to convince them to stop looking. The NPC has been abducted to be fed to the killer tree, and depending on what fits the situation, the NPC might still be with the gang, walking through the Zone with Brutus or trapped in the tree's tentacles.

◘ When the PCs talk to Ester she alternates between her regular self and her monotonous pod self. If the PCs comment on this she says she has been sleeping badly and that she dreams of tentacles and being covered by bark.

◘ An epilogue: A seed pod lies dead, face down, somewhere in the Zone. From the back of its head, a fresh green sprout rises towards the sunlight.

THE FAMILY HOMESTEAD

OVERVIEW

In a landscape of crumbling ruins sits a perfectly intact house from the Old Age. The homestead is surrounded by a high wooden fence and a barbed wire fence. Through a massive iron gate the building itself is visible: a large white brick house with thick, closed iron shutters. Behind the iron gate, a few dogs are growling menacingly as they try to push their wide jaws through the gate's bars. Behind them a green, several meter high reptile (a T-Rex) can be seen, gaping stiffly to reveal a maw filled with sharp fangs. Up close it turns out the huge reptile is made of plastic and is bolted to the ground.

Those that dare peek in through the gate can see a driveway where an armored car and a camper, also armored, are parked. In the garden on the other side of the house, a ragged blue and yellow flag twists in the wind on a flagpole. Usually one or several of the house's inhabitants are in or around the garden. Perhaps they're sitting down for a meal in the worn white plastic garden furniture.

THE SITUATION

The inhabitants of the homestead – nine non-mutated humans – are all descendants from a few families that decided to keep living their normal lives after the Apocalypse, above ground. It appears that they have been able to preserve their ancestors' lifestyle. They mow the lawn, take their dogs for walks, maintain their house and go shopping in abandoned stores in the Zone. Just like families in the Old Ages, they celebrate Christmas and go away on vacation in their caravan. At night the Family, as the inhabitants of the homestead prefer to call themselves, gather around the kitchen table to play board games and listen to scratchy old records playing on a wind-up record player.

However, the idyllic appearance is deceiving. The people of the homestead are anything but peaceful. Life in the Zone has turned them into bizarre and brutal cannibals. The Family is led by a married couple in their 60s, Mommie Dearest Sveah and Daddy Dearest Ragnar, who are also half-siblings. Below them in the strict family hierarchy are the seven Children, between 15 and 45 years old. Some of them are truly children of Sveah and Ragnar, others are siblings or half-siblings to their "parents". Ragnar also has children with his two daughters. No one in the Family consider this strange.

Visitors soon realize that all is not what it seems. The mood of the homestead is tightly wound and overly, even hysterically, affectionate. Sveah and Ragnar suddenly act hostile towards the Children. An attentive guest might also notice a macabre detail: a large glass jar in the kitchen contains hundreds of human teeth, teeth from guests and passers-by that the Family has eaten over the years. It's a habit they do not intend to give up. In a few places in the Zone they have built advanced traps designed to catch new, succulent victims.

INHABITANTS

Daddy Dearest Ragnar and Mommie Dearest Sveah and the seven Children: Hobbled Harry, Big Barbro, Sweet Lena, Olle the Hat, King Lotto, Lillemor and Little Brother. They are all cockeyed and weirdly similar-looking. In the summer, they all walk around in patched, blue tracksuits. In the winter they wear ski suits, knitted caps and heavy jackets. They never

leave the house unarmed and socialize almost exclusively within the group (the loner Hobbled Harry is the only exception). In the garden of the homestead there are five aggressive pitbulls, lovingly cared for by all the members of the Family.

Three interesting NPCs:

Daddy Dearest Ragnar, head of the Family. Cockeyed, elderly man. Tallest of the Family. Laughs loudly at his own jokes. Loves talking and dreaming about different marinades. Would like to be perceived as an easy-going joker, but is quick to menacing anger. Smells strongly of sweet, flowery perfume. Can usually be found in the kitchen, the garage or out in the Zone hunting for food.

Attributes: Strength 3, Agility 3, Wits 4, Empathy 2.
Skills: Escape 2, Shoot 3, Comprehend 2, Scout 3, Know the Zone 3, Manipulate 2.
Non-mutated.

Gear: Hunting rifle, bottle of perfume, soda can, three days' rations of cat food.

Hobbled Harry, loner and barbecue master. Tall, thin and cockeyed. Very similar-looking to his brother Ragnar. Always wears a chef's hat. Limps after battling a flock of zone rats. Obsessed with collecting knick-knacks. Often wanders the Zone alone with a shopping cart. Loves grilled meat and will do anything to get hold of barbecue gear. Gullible. Often licks his lips.

Attributes: Strength 4, Agility 4, Wits 1, Empathy 2.
Skills: Fight 2, Scout 3, Comprehend 2, Know the Zone 3.
Non-mutated.

Gear: Baseball bat, hunting knife, shopping cart, fanny pack filled with a variety of barbecue condiments.

Big Barbro, big sister. Tall girl wearing a ragged baseball cap and a stained pink t-shirt. Smells strongly of fried food. Stutters when she speaks. Extremely curious and inquisitive. Often laughs loudly and shrilly at nothing in particular. Harbors an intense hatred for the Parents but worships her younger siblings Lillemor and Little Brother. Has decided to find out more about the Zone. However, she only reluctantly leaves the homestead unless she is accompanied by dogs and siblings.

Attributes: Strength 5, Agility 3, Wits 3, Empathy 2.
Skills: Fight 2, Shoot 2, Know the Zone 2, Sense Emotion 2.
Non-mutated.

Gear: brass knuckles, hunting rifle, sunglasses, soda can.

THE FAMILY HOMESTEAD

GARDEN

COSY CORNER

KITCHEN

CAR & TRAILER

ARTIFACTS

Apart from what is visible outside the house (the plastic dinosaur, the car, the caravan) there is a plethora of items inside the house and the garage. A selection: map of the Zone, two hunting rifles, three hand grenades, 300 soda cans, 30 cans of gasoline, 10 bullets, five batteries, a plastic Christmas tree (with glitter, a star and red ornaments), a generator, four shopping carts, ten bottles of perfume, a refrigerator, a safe (locked, with three gold bars inside), a microwave, five paintings of idyllic landscape scenes (a backlit moose and similar motifs) and assorted furniture of varying condition (couch, armchairs, table, bookshelf, beds, chairs, etc).

GRUB AND WATER

In the kitchen there is a big water container (50 daily rations). In a freezer in the basement there's food (100 daily rations, 50 of which are human flesh). In the basement there are also canned goods (20 daily rations). The supplies are replenished irregularly.

EVENTS

The Family can be both ravenous enemies and bizarre allies. Since they have a car and know the Zone well they can show up far from home. The following events however are tied to the homestead:

- The PCs meet the Family in the street outside the homestead. They have just been "shopping". Their shopping carts are filled with artifacts. Perhaps the PCs want them to share? Most of the content of the carts happen to be things the PCs need right now.
- A large cage has been constructed on Daddy Dearest Ragnar's orders. It hangs from a chain next to the front door, and currently holds a new "morsel": a fully grown stalker from the PCs' Ark. She is a bit dazed and asks the PCs for help, but it will be hard to get her out without someone in the Family noticing.
- The PCs have become acquainted with the Family and have been invited to their house for dinner. Of course the Family has an ulterior motive: they either want to eat the PCs or, if it seems strategically sound, make them allies, perhaps to finish off a common enemy.

01

If the Family has cannibalistic intentions, they will attempt to sedate the PCs with ground-up sleeping pills dissolved in fine wine.

▫ Mommie Dearest Sveah has – erroneously or not – the impression that the PCs know and approve of the Family's cannibalism. She suggests that the PC deliver live "goods" in exchange for a few treasures (perhaps grub or a few cans of gasoline) from the homestead.

▫ The PCs have been aware of the Family for some time. Big Barbro has decided to kill the Parents, but is too afraid of the other members of the Family to do the deed on her own. She invites the PCs to the house when no one else is at home and offers them a generous reward to help her. She also proposes to two of the PCs at the same time (polygamy appeals to her).

LONG JOURNEYS

The Zone is big, far bigger than the People of the Ark can imagine. The area covered by the zone map is only a fraction of the Zone's endless expanse. The Zone is the world.

For some reason, the PCs might want to go on a longer journey, far beyond the edges of the zone map. Perhaps they have heard rumors of another settlement far, far away. Perhaps they think they can find Eden there. Perhaps they are running for their lives.

LARGE-SCALE MAP

To make a long journey you need a map with a larger scale than the Zone map. Instead of each square of the map being one mile across, it should be 20 miles. A single grid on this map is almost as big as the area covered by a normal zone map.

You can handle a longer journey almost exactly like any trek through the zone. Each grid on the map is equal to about one day's travel on foot. If the PCs have some sort of animal to ride or a vehicle they can normally cover two grids in one day. They move considerably faster than on a usual trek through the zone, because the object of a longer journey is simply travel, not to stop and explore. If the PCs want to stop and explore an area closer you should go back to using a normal zone map.

SECTOR ENVIRONMENT

You can create every grid on the larger map just like a normal sector in the Zone, with a few modifications. First of all, it is likely that most of the sectors will consist of wilderness. If you want to roll for the environment, use this table instead of the one on page 156 of *Mutant: Year Zero*. Roll D66:

11–16	Thick and dark forest. **Threats:** Yes. **Artifacts:** No.
21–26	Sparse and barren forest. **Threats:** Yes. **Artifacts:** No.
31–35	Windswept expanse of shrubbery. **Threats:** Yes. **Artifacts:** No.
36–42	Unnaturally verdant lands. **Threats:** Yes. **Artifacts:** No.
43–52	Desert of ashes and gravel. **Threats:** Yes. **Artifacts:** No.
53–54	Fields of shattered glass. **Threats:** Yes. **Artifacts:** No.
55–56	Gigantic crater. **Threats:** Yes. **Artifacts:** No.
61–65	Ruins of a city. **Threats:** Yes. **Artifacts:** Yes.
66	Settlement. Pick a specific zone sector.

Of course the environment within a grid may vary, the table only gives the most predominant conditions.

Ruins: If the sector environment is "Ruins of a city" you can randomly select or simple choose a few suitable ruins in the usual way (page 157 in *Mutant: Year Zero*). In other environments there may be some scattered ruins – that is up to you as Game master.

Rot levels are determined in the usual way (see table on page 125 of *Mutant: Year Zero*), with one difference: If you roll Zone oasis (Rot level zero), the whole grid is not rot free, it just means that there is a Zone oasis somewhere within it. The rest of the grid has rot level 1.

The Zone Stalker can Find the Path in the usual way when he enters a new grid on the map. However, it is impossible to rush through the grid in a shorter time so the last entry in the list on page 56 of *Mutant: Year Zero* cannot be chosen.

Artifacts: You can let the PCs find artifacts even if the roll on the table states that there are none. You rule the Zone! However, the zone stalker cannot choose to find artifacts in these grids as a Stunt of Find the Path.

MONSTER GENERATOR

The monsters found in chapter 13 of *Mutant: Year Zero* are enough for several game sessions. But it is very easy to create more weird animals and monsters for the players to tussle with. The monster generator below can create unique creatures from a number of tables and a handful of dice. Remember that you can just as easily choose a result or simply reroll if you think the result of your initial roll doesn't work. Sometimes contradictory results can create unexpected combinations, a feeble-minded herbivore with the attribute Bloodthirsty may appear to be peacefully chewing the cud when it suddenly becomes a mutant-eating monstrosity!

SIZE (D66)

11–14	Puny (Strength 1)
15–21	Small (Strength 2)
22–33	Average (Strength 3)
34–44	Massive (Strength 4)
45–55	Enormous (Strength 8)
56–62	Huge (Strength 10)
53–66	Gargantuan (Strength 12)

TYPE (D66)

11–18	Sluggish herbivore (Agility 0)
19–28	Herbivore (Agility 1)
29–36	Gatherer (Agility 2)
37–44	Scavenger (Agility 4)
45–62	Predator (Agility 6)
63–66	Aggressive predator (Agility 8)

LIMBS (2D6)

2–3	None
4–5	Two legs
6–7	Four legs
8–9	Wings
10	Six legs
11	Two legs, two arms
12	A multitude!

BODY/PROTECTION (2D6)

2–3	Skin
4–5	Soft fur
6–7	Thick fur (armor 1)
8–9	Scales (armor 2)
10	Shell (armor 4)
11	Bone plates (armor 6)
12	Armored skin (armor 8)

WEAPONS (D66)

11–16	Claws (Strength 1–3 damage 1, Strength 4–8 damage 2, Strength 9+ damage 3)
21–26	Bite (Strength 1–3 damage 1, Strength 4–5 damage 2, Strength 6+ damage 3)
31–34	Venomous bite (Roll 1D6: 1–3 Nerve Poison, 4–6 Hallucinogenic Poison, see page 183 of *Mutant: Year Zero*)
35–36	Acid spit (Range: Near, damage 1)
41–46	Kick (Strength 1–3 damage 1, Strength 4–8 damage 2, Strength 9+ damage 3)
51–56	Horns (Strength 1–3 damage 1, Strength 4–5 damage 2, Strength 6–8 damage 3, Strength 9+ damage 4)
61–65	Roll twice
66	Unique

01

SKILLS (D66)

Not all monsters have skills, those that have no skill levels only roll their Base Dice.

11–26	No skills
31–36	Move
41–56	As weapon (Fight for melee weapons, Shoot for ranged weapons)
61–64	As weapon + Move
65–66	As weapon + Move + Endure

SKILL LEVEL (D66)

Roll once for each skill.

11–26	Skill Level 1
31–46	Skill Level 2
51–56	Skill Level 3
61–65	Skill Level 4
66	Skill Level 5

NUMBERS (2D6)

2–3	Flock (4D6 creatures)
4–5	Pack (2D6 creatures)
6–9	Loner
10–11	Family (1D6 creatures)
12	Swarm (+3 Strength, can only be damaged by flamethrowers and mutations)

LOCATION (D66)

11–16	Burrow
21–26	Ruin
31–36	Water hole
41–46	Tree/high ground
51–56	Wreck
61–66	Crater

MUTATIONS (OPTIONAL)

Monsters generally have no mutations in *Mutant: Year Zero* but there is nothing stopping you from creating your own mutated monsters. The basic principle is that the monsters begins with 1 MP for every mutation it has. Mutated monsters can also Push like any other mutant. Roll 1D6:

1–3	No mutation
4	One mutation
5	Two mutations
6	Three mutations

TRAITS (D66)

11	Affectionate
12	Timid
13	Reeking
14	Hoarder
15	Aggressive
16	Colorful
21	Playful
22	Starving
23	Wounded
24	In heat
25	Slimy
26	Bloodthirsty
31	Intelligent
32	Horrifying
33	Sleepy
34	Irritated
35	Lonely
36	Curious
37	Roaring
38	Rot-afflicted
39	Scrawny
40	Fat
41	Fast
42	Motherly
43	Confused
44	Insane
45	Stressed
46	Dejected
51	Scabbed
52	Chewer
53	Cute
54	Ugly
55	Stupid
56	Lazy
61–65	Roll twice
66	Machine

NAME (D66 TWICE)

Zone monsters are unlikely to have well-known names, but Zone Stalkers like naming the strange beasts they come across in the Zone. A PC that succeeds on a simple roll of Know the Zone can, in most cases, recall a name whispered around the campfires in the Ark.

D66	PREFIX
11	Lurk-
12	Soot-
13	Scorch-
14	Blight-
15	Snapper-
16	Razor-
21	Thunder-
22	Blister-
23	Gore-
24	Earth-
25	Rock-
26	Water-
31	Dune-
32	Bog-
33	Storm-
34	Stink-
35	Blood-
36	Taint-
41	Copper-
42	Iron-
43	Steel-
44	Rot-
45	Scrap-
46	Howl-
51	Burst-
52	Steppe-
53	Slate-
54	Salt-
55	Grin-
56	Sugar-
61	Whisper-
62	Sickle-
63	Glow-
64	Reaper-

D66	PREFIX
65	Doom-
66	Burrow-

D66	SUFFIX
11	-toad
12	-swine
13	-hound
14	-swarm
15	-glider
16	-blob
21	-owl
22	-bat
23	-roller
24	-ling
25	-raptor
26	-wraith
31	-fish
32	-worm
33	-rodent
34	-sponge
35	-flower
36	-cat
41	-crawler
42	-ape
43	-slug
44	-dancer
45	-bug
46	-vermin
51	-behemoth
52	-gnat
53	-eater
54	-stalker
55	-orb
56	-flapper
61	-adder
62	-monster
63	-hawk
64	-bird
65	-leech
66	-lizard

Name:

Role:

Appearance:

Goal:

ATTRIBUTES

Strength	Damage	○○○○○
Agility	Fatigue	○○○○○
Wits	Confusion	○○○○○
Empathy	Doubt	○○○○○

SKILLS

TALENTS

MUTATIONS

MUTATION POINTS

○○○○○○○○○○

WEAPONS, ARTIFACTS & GEAR

Name:

Role:

Appearance:

Goal:

ATTRIBUTES

Strength	Damage	○○○○○
Agility	Fatigue	○○○○○
Wits	Confusion	○○○○○
Empathy	Doubt	○○○○○

SKILLS

TALENTS

MUTATIONS

MUTATION POINTS

○○○○○○○○○○

WEAPONS, ARTIFACTS & GEAR

Name:

Role:

Appearance:

Goal:

ATTRIBUTES

Strength	Damage	○○○○○
Agility	Fatigue	○○○○○
Wits	Confusion	○○○○○
Empathy	Doubt	○○○○○

SKILLS

TALENTS

MUTATIONS

MUTATION POINTS

○○○○○○○○○○

WEAPONS, ARTIFACTS & GEAR